Casey's Unexpected Friend
by Kate Stormer
Illustrated by Tom Lowes

Goblin Fern Press
Madison, Wisconsin

Casey's Unexpected Friend
Text Copyright © 2003 Kate Stormer
Illustrations Copyright © 2003 Tom Lowes

For information or to order additional copies please contact

Goblin Fern Press, Inc.

3809 Mineral Point Road, Madison, WI 53705

Toll-free: 888-670-BOOK (2665)   www.goblinfernpress.com

ISBN: 0-9722099-7-2

Printed in the United States
First Goblin Fern Press Edition: July 2003
10 9 8 7 6 5 4 3 2 1

Casey's World™

Welcome to Casey's World!
Casey would love to hear from you.

Please write to
Casey
c/o Goblin Fern Press
or email her directly at
Casey@caseysworld.net

You can also visit her at
www.caseysworld.net
to find out about new adventures!

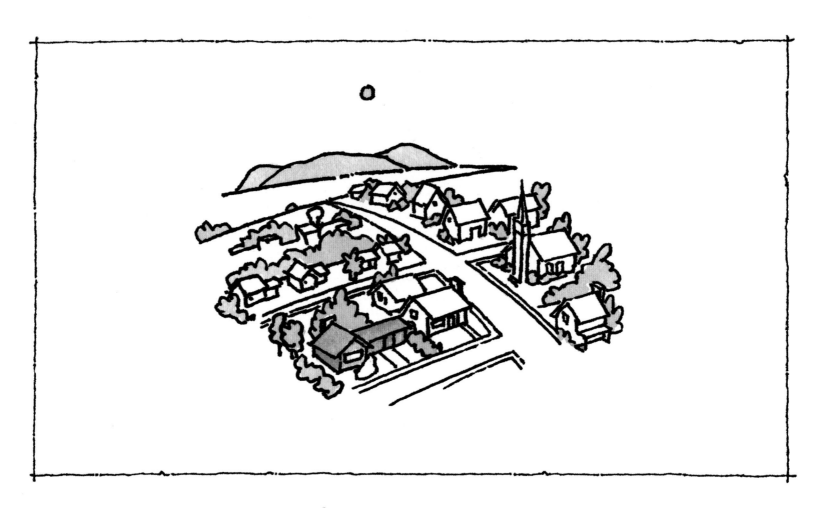

On a very quiet street
in a very quiet town
lived a very noisy little dog.

Her name was Casey.
She was small and gray and soft to touch.

Casey lived in a blue house with a big rock in the front yard.
Neighborhood children loved to stop by Casey's house to play on the big rock,
and she would watch them from her favorite chair next to
the huge front window.

"Hey, be careful," Casey would say to the boys and girls as they climbed on the rock. "You might fall down and get hurt."

Casey was proud of how well she protected all the playful children.
Her mother would tell her she did a fine job
asking all the boys and girls to be careful on the big rock.
Then she would give Casey a doggie snack and a pat on the head.
"Life is wonderful," thought Casey.

One day Casey's mother came home from work with something in her arms.
The thing that was wrapped in the blanket wiggled and squiggled.
Suddenly, a tiny black nose and two bright eyes appeared from under the blanket.
It was a puppy.

The puppy did not look like Casey at all.
It had red curly fur that did not feel soft like Casey's.
"I do not like you," Casey said to the puppy.
"You do not look like me, and you are bigger than me."
Casey heard her mother call the little puppy Reba,
and decided that she would never like this curly, red puppy named Reba.
Never!

Casey crept to the corner without saying another word to Reba.
What if her mother liked Reba better than she liked Casey?
Even worse, what if her mother stopped loving Casey altogether?
And what if the children liked Reba more than they liked her?

"That would not be good," thought Casey.
"This is MY mother and MY rock and MY children.
I do not want Reba at my house."

For the whole summer, Reba grew and grew.
Soon she was very big and wanted to play all the time.
Casey's mother played tug with Reba.
And one day, Reba even tried to play tug with Casey.

"Go away," Casey growled at Reba.
"I don't want to play with you. I don't like you,
and I wish you would just go away."

Reba even had her very own food bowl that looked just like Casey's.
Casey was not happy any more and did not like this puppy at all.
"I wish Reba had never come to live with us," thought Casey.

One day while Casey was on her chair by the window, the school bus stopped
in front of the house. Casey noticed a new little girl getting off the bus.
She was quieter than all the other children, and when the others ran to climb on the rock,
the little girl just stood watching.
"Be careful," Casey told the children playing. "Be very careful."

Soon all the children went home, except for the small girl.
She went to the big rock and began to climb on it.

"Don't climb on the rock," Casey barked in her loudest voice.
"It is too big for someone as small as you."
But the little girl did not hear Casey.
She just kept climbing and climbing.

"You are too high," yowled Casey even louder than before.
But the girl still did not stop.
She did not even look over to Casey as the other children always did.
"She can't hear me!" Casey suddenly realized.

And then it happened. The little girl started to fall off the big rock.
"Oh no," cried Casey.
"She is falling, and I'm too small to jump out the window to help her."

Suddenly, the tiny girl stopped falling.
Her coat had gotten caught on the edge of the rough rock.
"What should I *do*?" whimpered Casey.
"She will fall and get hurt if someone doesn't save her."

Then Casey had a great idea.
She rushed to where Reba was taking a nap.
"Reba, wake up!" Casey barked loudly.
"You are big, and you can reach the open window.
Please jump through it and run to the big rock to save the little girl."

Reba rushed to the window and jumped up ... up ... and
right through the open window.

She raced across the front yard and right up to the girl.
Reba grabbed the little girl by her coat sleeve with her mouth and
gently placed her on the soft grass.
Then she gave the little girl a big puppy kiss on the cheek.

The little girl laughed, and Reba wagged her tail very fast.
"She is OK," sighed Casey.
"Reba saved the little girl."

When it was time to go to bed that night,
Casey and Reba each went to their soft pillows that were right next to each other.

"Thanks for keeping the rock safe for all the children today,"
Casey said quietly to Reba.
And Casey cuddled closer to Reba than she had ever been before.

Reba, with her nose very close to Casey's ear, whispered,
"I hope someday I will be just like you, Casey.
You are the best at keeping all the children safe, and I love you."
And then Reba drifted off to sleep.

"Life is wonderful," said Casey.
And then she, too, fell fast asleep.

Ponder Points

"My Ponder Points are intended to inspire discussions and questions, boost creativity and spark imaginations. I hope they will help each child to better understand and enjoy my adventures, whether they read them or listen to them."

Have you ever helped someone?
How did you help? How did you feel when you helped?

Can someone love more than one person...or dog? Who do you love?

Why didn't Casey want a new puppy coming into her home?

Are you different than your friends?
How are you different? Is it OK to be different?

Why do you think the little girl just watched and didn't play with the other children?
Do you sometimes feel like the little girl?

Why do you think the little girl didn't hear Casey?
Do you know anyone who cannot hear? What would it be like to not hear?

Did you know that some dogs are big and some are small?
What can you do when you are small? What can you do when you are big?

Do you think Casey liked Reba at the end of the story?
Are they friends? Who are your friends? Who would you like to be your friends?

BOOK ORDER FORM

Please copy this page to order Casey's Unexpected Friend

☐ YES! I would like to order CASEY'S UNEXPECTED FRIEND

Name _____

Address _____

City_____ State_____ Zip_____

Phone _____

Email _____

Quantity ordering _____ x $16^{95} = $_____

Wisconsin Residents add 5.5% Sales Tax = $_____

ISBN: 0-9722099-7-2

Shipping and Handling first book $5^{00} = $_____

Shipping and Handling each additional book $1^{50} = $_____

TOTAL $_____

All orders pre-paid please!

☐ By credit card: ☐ VISA ☐ Mastercard Card #:_____ - _____ - _____ - _____

Expiration Date: _____ Signature_____

☐ By check: Payable to **Goblin Fern Press**
3809 Mineral Point Road
Madison, WI 53705

Orders may be submitted by mail, fax or through our secure website, **www.goblinfernpress.com**.

Toll-free: 888-670-BOOK (2665) • Tel: 608-442-0212 • Fax: 608-442-0221 • Email: info@goblinfernpress.com